FINDING FIZZ

White Wolves Series Consultant: Sue Ellis,
Centre for Literacy in Primary Education

This book can be used in the White Wolves Guided Reading programme
with children who have an average level of reading experience at Year 4 level

First published 2006 by
A & C Black Publishers Ltd
38 Soho Square, London, W1D 3HB

www.acblack.com

Text copyright © 2006 J. Alexander
Illustrations copyright © 2006 Cherry Whytock

ISBN 0-7136-7625-6
ISBN 978-0-7136-7625-9

A CIP catalogue for this book is available from the British Library.

A & C Black uses paper produced with elemental chlorine-free
pulp, harvested from managed sustained forests.

Printed and bound in Great Britain by Bookmarque Ltd, Croydon

FINDING FIZZ

J. Alexander

illustrated by Cherry Whytock

A & C Black • London

CONTENTS

CHAPTER ONE

"I never noticed what fat ankles you've got!" Jax said.

The rest of the gang laughed.

Carly could feel her face going red. She shouldn't have worn a skirt. She didn't like skirts anyway, but when Jax said: "Let's all wear skirts tomorrow", they just did.

Carly forced herself to laugh with the others.

Their teacher, Miss Fenn, called them the Funny Five because they were always giggling, and they called her Miss Piggy, but not to her face, of course.

Sam   Suse   Carly   Becca   Jax

They had secret nicknames
for everyone, like Mopey Mo
for Maisie, who
used to be one
of the gang
until she went
blubbing to
the head
teacher. All
they'd done
was stop
talking to her.
It had only
been a bit of fun.

Now they were poking fun at
Carly's fat ankles.

They stopped people sitting
in the empty chair next to her
at lunch to give her plenty of
legroom.

They kept looking under the
table to check if her ankles were
growing.

They pretended to be scared in
case her ankles got enormous and
blew up.

That evening, Carly looked
at her legs in
the mirror.

Maybe
they were
a bit fat.

Jax was as thin as a stick,
with sleek black hair down to
her shoulders. She was the
best-looking girl in school
and everyone knew it.

Carly wanted to go back to wearing trousers, so no one could see her fat ankles any more. But then everyone would laugh at her for trying to hide them. All she could do was wait for the teasing to stop.

In Jax's gang, someone was always being teased and when it was your turn you just had to put up with it.

Sooner or later, Jax would get bored and start picking on someone else instead.

But this time, the teasing went on and on, and Carly found it harder and harder not to let it get to her. Finally, she did the one thing Jax simply couldn't stand – she got upset.

They called her a crybaby, then they stopped talking to her altogether.

They passed notes to each other in class, leaving her out. They whispered things behind their hands and giggled.

When one of the notes fell on
the floor, Carly picked it up. Suse
had drawn a girl with tree trunks
for legs, Sam had added a green
branch to one of
them and Becca
had put a bird's
nest on it. Jax
had written 'tree
trunks!!' at
the bottom.

TREE TRUNKS !!

They had given her a
nickname! They weren't supposed
to do that to someone in the gang.
Nicknames were only for sad
losers outside it.

Carly was shocked and hurt.

She wanted to go off on her own and hide.

Somehow she got through the rest of the afternoon, but when the bell went she still had to go home on the same bus as Jax and Sam.

Perhaps she was imagining it, but it seemed as if everyone stopped talking when she got on the bus.

As she brushed past a boy in her class, he yelled, "Ouch! I think I've got a splinter!"

All the kids laughed – even some that Carly hardly knew. Her so-called friends must have told everyone her so-called secret nickname and now the whole school was laughing at her behind her back.

Carly's face felt hot. She sat bolt upright and stared straight ahead until the

first stop. Then she got off to walk the last mile home.

Instead of going in right away, Carly slipped into the alley behind her house to try and calm down. She didn't want her mum to see she had been crying.

It was then she heard it. A whimper, like an animal in pain. Putting her bag on the ground, Carly bent down and very gently parted the hedge.

CHAPTER TWO

When she was little, Carly had been mad about dogs, but her mum had always told her to stay away from strays. Unless you knew an animal well, she said, you could never tell whether it might bite.

The little dog lying in a heap under the garden hedge was in no state to bite anyone.

Carly reached out to stroke him, slowly, letting him see and smell her hand first. His body was so thin she could see the hard ridges of his ribs under the wiry, brown fur.

She took off her sweatshirt and spread it out on the path. Then she slipped her hands under the little stray dog and lifted him gently out from under the hedge. She put him

on the sweatshirt and wrapped him up in it.

Carly's mum came out of her study as soon as she heard the back door. "I've just had a call from Miss Fenn. She's worried about you…" She stopped. "What have you got there?"

Carly showed her. "I found him under our hedge," she said.

To her surprise, Mum didn't go nuts that she'd picked up a stray dog.

"Poor little thing," she said. "He looks as if he hasn't eaten for a month. Let's see if he'll take a drink of water."

Carly sat on the floor beside

the dog, while her mum filled a shallow dish from the kitchen tap.

At first, the little dog didn't seem to be interested, but when Carly dipped her fingers into the water he licked it off, and then suddenly he seemed to notice how thirsty he was. He pulled himself up and drank straight from the bowl.

Carly's mum found a cold sausage in the fridge. She chopped it up with some milk and the little dog ate it hungrily. As soon as he had finished, he lay down and shut his eyes. He seemed to be worn out by the effort of eating.

Carly's mum said he had probably just got lost. He was hungry and tired, and maybe also sad because he was missing his owner.

"He's lost his fizz," she said, stroking his side with her finger. "A bit like you, Carly. That's what Miss Fenn was phoning about. She's noticed you don't seem to be your usual happy self at the moment. Actually, I've noticed that, too."

In the excitement of finding the little dog, Carly had forgotten about Jax and the gang. She didn't want to tell her mum about it because it was only a bit of teasing and people should be able to handle that for themselves.

"It's not a good idea to bottle things up," her mum said. "You don't have to tell me if you don't want to, but you should talk to someone. It'll make you feel better."

Carly shrugged. Taking the little dog with her, she went to lie down on the sofa. He curled up on her tummy, warm and heavy.

She gently stroked his back until
he fell asleep.

"What's the point of talking?"
she said softly. And then she told
him everything. When she had
finished, she let out a sigh.

"That's the way it is in Jax's
gang," she said. "If you're the one
that's getting cut out, you just
have to take it until it blows over."

Except it still hadn't blown over with Maisie. She had blubbed, and they had never let her back in. Now Carly had blubbed, and maybe they would never let her back in, either.

CHAPTER THREE

"Did you hear she got off the bus early?" Jax said to the others, talking about Carly as if she wasn't there. "I think she fancied a walk!"

They all laughed.

Carly told herself that if she hadn't got off the bus early and walked home in tears and ducked into the back alley to dry her eyes,

then she would never have found
the little stray dog. That helped
her to feel better.

All day, whenever anyone was
horrible to her, Carly thought
about the little dog
waiting for her at
home and it made
her smile.

She remembered
his bright eyes shining up at her
in the dark kitchen when she had
gone down to check on him in the
night, and the way he'd wagged
his tail when she had come down
for breakfast in the morning. He
was already getting to know her.

She planned all sorts of nice
things they could do together once
he'd got his strength back. They
could play hide-and-seek in the
garden. She could
take him for walks
in the park.

The others didn't like to see her
sitting there, grinning to herself,
when they were trying to wind her
up, so they told Miss Fenn that she
was being horrible to them.

Miss Fenn didn't believe it, but she said it might be a good idea for Carly to move to another table.

"Serves her right," Jax hissed. "Now she'll have to sit with Mopey Mo."

"Losers," Maisie said, under her breath, as Carly sat down. "Don't take any notice of them."

Carly gave Maisie a fleeting smile but she didn't want to be too friendly to her because then she'd certainly never get back in with the Funny Five. Miss Fenn would have to rename them the Funny Four. Though that still sounded good.

She bent over her books, pretending to be hard at work so that everyone would stop looking at her.

When I get out of here, she thought, I'll go to the shop and buy some dog biscuits. I'll ask Mrs Arnold if she's got any cardboard boxes in the storeroom that I can have. Then I'll put them round the kitchen and hide one biscuit in each box, so my little dog will want to get up and go looking for them…

She thought about this plan all the way back home in the bus. It kept her going. At last, the bus stopped outside the village shop, and Carly got off. But as she was opening the door she noticed a card in the window:

Small white-and-
brown dog found
wandering in
MaidenLane.
Please call·····

It was her telephone number!
What if someone had already seen
the card and come to claim him?

Carly forgot about her
shopping and ran home as fast
as she could.

"What have you done?" she
shouted at her mum as soon as she
opened the door. She dashed into
the kitchen, making the little dog
yelp in surprise.

Carly's mum told her to sit down and calm down. She said she had put a card in the village shop and a small ad in the paper.

"We can't just keep the dog," she said. "His real owner will be missing him. I thought you understood that, Carly."

Carly did understand, but she didn't want to. She told herself that the dog's real owners didn't deserve to have him back. She tried to convince herself that as they had been careless enough to lose him in the first place maybe they wouldn't bother to come looking for him now.

CHAPTER FOUR

The next day, Carly went back to sitting in her usual place with Jax and the gang, but they were still ignoring her.

When she tried to talk to them they just looked at each other and said, "Did you hear something?"

Carly tried to cheer herself up
by thinking about the
little dog, but it didn't
work. Now he was just
something else to
worry about, another
friend she was probably going
to lose.

Right
at this
very
minute,
someone
could be
knocking
at the
door.

Someone could be picking him up and taking him away, and she

wouldn't even have a chance to say goodbye.

At playtime, when everyone went outside, Carly stayed sitting at her desk. She didn't understand why her friends had turned against her. It didn't feel like a joke any more; it felt really nasty. She couldn't believe that it had all started because she had fat ankles.

It wasn't as if she could help that and, anyway, what difference did it make to anyone else what shape her legs were?

"Do you want a crisp?"

It was Maisie.

Carly looked at the bag of crisps she was holding out and hesitated for a moment.

Then she shook her head. Maisie took a bunch of crisps and put them in her mouth.

"This is how you must have felt when we were all being horrible to you," Carly said. "I'm so sorry."

"You'll get over it," said Maisie. "I did."

Carly suddenly realised that although the group still called her Mopey Mo, it was ages since Maisie had actually got upset at school. She hadn't made many new friends, but that didn't seem to bother her.

"Sure you don't want a crisp?"

Carly took one. It seemed like the sign Maisie had been waiting for.

"You know what I think?" she said. "I think you should move on to my table full time. That would show them."

Carly thought about it. Then she slowly nodded. Why not? What had she got to lose? She used to get on really well with Maisie before Jax had turned everyone against her, and she suddenly realised how much she had missed her.

The two girls went to find Miss Fenn.

Sitting next to Maisie, it was good to see that she was doing her weird little doodles again, building up detailed pictures and then hiding things in them that didn't  belong – a cherry cake in a busy street, an alarm clock in a playground.

Maisie was good at drawing, but she'd given it up when Jax had said art was for saddos.

"Would you like to come to my house after school?" Carly asked.

Maisie shrugged. "OK," she said.

So that afternoon, Carly had someone to sit beside on the bus and it was easier to ignore Jax and Sam, whispering in the seat behind.

When she opened the back
gate, the little dog was waiting for
her in the garden. He bounded up,
barking joyfully. It was amazing
how much better
he was after
just a few
days.

"I didn't know you had a dog!"
said Maisie. "What's his name?"

Carly told Maisie that the dog didn't have a name. "We haven't had him very long," she said.

She didn't want to admit that they might not be keeping him very long, either.

"He's got to have a name!" said Maisie.

They talked about names for a bit and then gave up because they couldn't think of a good one. Then they played ball with the dog until he buried it.

Lying on the lawn in the sunshine, Carly decided to trust Maisie and tell her the truth. "The trouble is," she said. "The dog isn't really mine. I found him."

"Where?"

"Under the hedge. Mum says if no one comes to claim him before Saturday then we'll know he's been abandoned and I can keep him."

"But that's great," Maisie said.

"It's a long time till Saturday," said Carly.

CHAPTER FIVE

Jax and the gang tried to stop
Carly being friends with Maisie.

"She
wants to
watch out,"
they said.
"Or she'll
get stuck
with
Mopey Mo
for ever."

They were still talking about her as if she wasn't there.

When that didn't work, they started picking on both girls, calling them The Sisters of Sad.

Carly didn't care. All she could think about was her little dog, and how she still might lose him. But she was glad to have Maisie around, who knew what she was going through.

On Thursday afternoon, Jax told Carly she was having a sleepover. She had finally decided to let Carly back in the gang.

In the past, Carly would have gone crawling back gratefully, but not this time.

"Sorry, I'm doing something on Saturday," she said.

Jax couldn't have looked more surprised if Carly had slapped her with a wet kipper. For one thing, nobody ever knocked back Jax.

For another, she probably thought Carly hadn't got anything better to do with her time than sit around feeling miserable and left out.

"What?" said Jax, forgetting for once to be cool. "What are you doing?"

"Nothing you'd be interested in," said Carly.

It was great to see how much Jax couldn't bear not knowing!

So that Saturday afternoon, instead of going to the sleepover, Carly found herself walking to the park with the little dog – *her* little dog! She was meeting Maisie, and she was early because she was so happy and excited that she kept breaking into a run.

As soon as they got to the park,
Carly let her dog off the lead and
threw the ball for him.
He went after it …
but then he kept
on running.

"Hey!
Come back!"
yelled Carly, racing after him.

There was a group of kids
standing around the edge of the
skate park with sketchbooks,

drawing the skateboarders.
To Carly's horror, the little dog
launched himself into the middle
of them, barking joyfully, making
them jump and scatter.

"I'm sorry, I'm so sorry..."
Carly muttered, trying to grab
him.

The little dog stopped suddenly and looked up, wagging his tail so hard that he almost fell over. Maisie laughed and bent down, letting him lick her chin.

"I didn't know you did art classes!" said Carly.

Maisie picked up her things and the two girls made their way back across the grass towards the ice-cream kiosk. She told Carly that she had joined the art class to cheer herself up when Jax and the gang were being horrible to her, and now it was her favourite thing in the world.

"We're making a comic strip about a skateboard superstar this term. It's brilliant!"

"So that's why you stopped being mopey," said Carly. "That's how you found your fizz."

Maisie gave her a quizzical look and Carly explained.

"It's something my mum says when someone's feeling gloomy – she says they've lost their fizz. I lost my fizz when everyone started being nasty to me…"

"Well, you've found it now," said Maisie, bending down to pat the little dog.

"I know," said Carly. "I can't believe no one's come for him. Now we really must think of a name."

"Isn't it obvious?" said Maisie. "You must call him Fizz!"

Carly grinned. It was perfect. Everything was perfect – getting thrown out of the not-so-funny five, being friends with Maisie again and, best of all, finding Fizz.

ABOUT THE AUTHOR

Jen Alexander grew up in London but she always wanted to live by the sea, so she moved first to the Shetland Isles and then to North Cornwall, where she lives today.

Jen started writing about 12 years ago, when the youngest of her four children started school. She has written loads of books, both fiction and non fiction, for readers of every age, but she enjoys writing for juniors best!

Other White Wolves that raise issues...

Taking Flight

Julia Green

Luke loves visiting his grandad
and helping out with the pigeons.
But Grandad gets sick and
muddled and needs more than
Luke's help. When he goes into
hospital, events take a turn for
the worse and suddenly Luke
has to grow up very fast...

Taking Flight is a story about
love, loss and friendship.

ISBN: 0-7136-7594-2   £4.99

Other White Wolves that raise issues...

Nothing But Trouble

Alan MacDonald

It's a tough job for Paul being Jago's 'buddy' at school. The new boy comes from a family of travellers and he doesn't say much or seem interested in making friends. Then Paul discovers Jago has a secret and a special bond develops between the two boys, but how long can it last?

Nothing But Trouble is a story about prejudice and not fitting in.

ISBN: 0-7136-7679-5   £4.99

WHITE WOLVES